By the same author

Peedie Peebles' Summer or Winter Book

Katie Morag Delivers the Mail
Katie Morag and the Two Grandmothers
Katie Morag and the Tiresome Ted
Katie Morag and the Big Boy Cousins
Katie Morag and the New Pier

PEEDIE PEEBLES'
COLOUR
BOOK

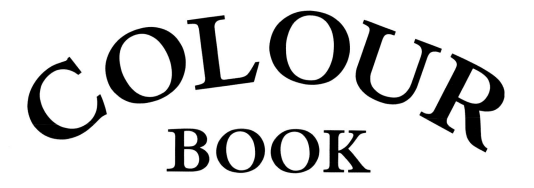

Mairi Hedderwick

THE BODLEY HEAD
London

1 3 5 7 9 10 8 6 4 2

Copyright © Mairi Hedderwick 1994

Mairi Hedderwick has asserted her right under the Copyright,
Designs and Patents Act, 1988 to be identified as the author and
illustrator of this work

First published in the United Kingdom 1994
by The Bodley Head Children's Books
Random House, 20 Vauxhall Bridge Road, London SW1V 2SA

Random House Australia (Pty) Limited
20 Alfred Street, Milsons Point, Sydney,
New South Wales 2061, Australia

Random House New Zealand Limited
18 Poland Road, Glenfield,
Auckland 10, New Zealand

Random House South Africa (Pty) Limited
PO Box 337, Bergvlei 2012, South Africa

Random House UK Limited Reg. No. 954009

A CIP catalogue record for this book is available
from the British Library

ISBN 0 370 31842 0

Designed by Rowan Seymour
Printed in Hong Kong

For Sophie

The Peebles family have just moved house. There's a lot of work to be done; the new house is very dull and dingy inside.

'Just needs a coat of paint, that's all,' they said.
Peedie Peebles went to find his paint brush.

'Peedie Peebles is *not* allowed to go near any of the paint pots,'
said Mum and Dad and big sister Bo.

Peedie Peebles was annoyed.

The hall was the first room to be painted.
'I like red,' said Mum.

'So does Peedie Peebles,' smiled the postie.
'Oh no, Peedie Peebles!'

The second room was the kitchen.
'I like yellow,' said Bo.

'So does Peedie Peebles,' laughed the milkman.
'Oh no, Peedie Peebles!'

The third room was the bathroom.
'I like blue,' said Dad.

'So does Peedie Peebles,' warned the bin man.
'Oh no, Peedie Peebles!'

The fourth room to be painted was the sitting room.
'I like orange,' said Mum.

'So does Peedie Peebles,' noticed the nosy neighbour.
'Oh no, Peedie Peebles!'

Mum and Dad's bedroom was the fifth room.
'We love green,' they said.

'So does Peedie Peebles,' said the nice neighbour.
'Oh no, Peedie Peebles!'

The sixth room to be painted belonged to Bo.
'I love purple,' she said.

'I'm tired,' said Mum. 'Only one room left,' said Dad.
'The last room to do is Peedie Peebles'.'

But Peedie Peebles' bedroom was *already* painted.

'I don't like this,' said Mum. 'Look at the mess,' said Dad.
'Oh *no*, Peedie Peebles!'

With a bit of help, Peedie Peebles' room was soon finished.

It was the best painted room in the whole house.
'Time for a bath,' said Mum.

'OH NO, Peedie Peebles . . . !'